ATTACK
OF THE
SHARK-HEADED
ZOMBIE

ATTACK
OF THE
SHARK-HEADED
ZOMBIE

by Bill Doyle
illustrated by Scott Altmann

A STEPPING STONE BOOK™
Random House 🏠 New York

To RSII and KMB. Zap those zombies!
—B.D.

For Dylan and Addie
—S.A.

Text copyright © 2011 by Bill Doyle
Cover art and interior illustrations copyright © 2011 by Scott Altmann

Visit us on the Web!
SteppingStonesBooks.com
www.randomhouse.com/kids

Educators and librarians, for a variety of teaching tools, visit us at
www.randomhouse.com/teachers

Library of Congress Cataloging-in-Publication Data
Doyle, Bill H.
Attack of the shark-headed zombie / by Bill Doyle ; illustrated by Scott Altmann. —
1st ed.
p. cm.
"A Stepping Stone Book."
Summary: In order to earn money for new bicycles, nine-year-old cousins Keats and Henry take a job at a very strange house where doors disappear, carpets bite, and a zombie shark comes after them.
ISBN 978-0-375-86675-3 (pbk.) — ISBN 978-0-375-96675-0 (lib. bdg.) —
ISBN 978-0-375-89813-6 (ebook)
[1. Magic—Fiction. 2. Zombies—Fiction. 3. Cousins—Fiction.
4. Moneymaking projects—Fiction.] I. Altmann, Scott, ill. II. Title.
PZ7.D7725 Att 2011
[Fic]—dc22   2010022539

Printed in the United States of America

10

CONTENTS

STUNT KIDS

"UGH!" KEATS GASPED. With one last shove, he pushed his bike to the top of Steep Cliff Hill. This was the highest spot around. He couldn't believe he'd made it!

As usual, his cousin Henry had climbed a lot faster. He sat waiting for Keats on a rock at the top.

"Ready for the ride of your life?" Henry asked with a grin. He jumped to his feet.

"Just a second," Keats said. He carefully brushed a few specks of dirt off Webster. That was what he called his bike. Keats liked Webster to shine, especially on sunny summer afternoons like today.

"Give your bike a bath later," Henry said, laughing. "You've got to see this." He pulled Keats over to look down the other side of the hill.

"Whoa," Keats said, and his stomach flip-flopped. The rocky slope ran straight down, almost like a wall. At the bottom, a cliff dropped into a deep lake.

"You want to ride our bikes down *that*?" Keats squinted up at Henry. The cousins were both nine, but Henry was two inches taller.

"You got it, cuz." Henry slapped him on the back. "My World's Greatest Plan is for us to be stunt kids in movies."

"Oh man," Keats groaned. "Not another one of your World's Greatest Plans! Remember when you said we should be snake dentists?"

"This time is different," Henry said. "If we spend the summer training to be stunt kids, we'll be famous by fall." He pointed down Steep Cliff Hill. "This will be our first mission. We just ride down and stop before the cliff."

Keats shook his head. "That's so nuts you should sell peanut butter."

"Nuts?" Henry asked. "It's totally safe." Then he scratched his chin. Keats knew his cousin well. Scratching his chin was a sure sign that Henry was lying.

Keats decided he would *not* ride down the scary side of Steep Cliff Hill. Sure, Henry would call him chicken for going back the easy way. But that was better than taking the chance that Webster might get scratched.

Besides, it was a perfect afternoon for shooting hoops. From up here Keats could see the basketball court in the park. And there! He spotted his other favorite place in their small town, the library. Maybe he'd drop by to see if any new books had come in.

Keats started to explain. "Henry, I'm going down—"

"Great!" Henry interrupted. "I knew you wouldn't let me ride alone. I'll go first!"

Before Keats could stop him, Henry hopped on his bike and zipped straight down Steep Cliff Hill. As if he'd done it a million times, he skidded to a halt right before the edge of the cliff.

"Come on, Keats!" Henry shouted from way below. "It's easy!"

It *did* look easy, Keats told himself. And he didn't want to let Henry down. Maybe he should just give it a try. He could always stop halfway if he got freaked out.

Keats touched his lucky baseball cap under his helmet and gave his bike a pat. "Let's go, Webster."

He started down the hill. Right away, Keats knew this was a huge mistake. The rocky ground made the wheels jitter and the handlebars shake. And Keats was going way too fast. He wanted to stop. He tried putting on the brakes—

Oh no!

His jeans were snagged in the gears. He couldn't press the pedals back to brake. He was completely out of control . . . and he was heading for the cliff.

"Henry!" Keats shouted. "I! Can't! Stop!"

In a flash, Henry dropped his own bike and ran a few feet up the hill. When Keats zoomed by, Henry yanked on his arm. Keats fell off the bike, his jeans tearing free. The boys tumbled onto the grass. But Webster kept going and smacked into Henry's bike. Both bikes flew over the cliff and spun through the air end over end.

Keploosh!

The bikes splashed into the deep lake and sank. Keats looked from the edge of the cliff to his cousin, who grinned.

"Why are you smiling?" Keats demanded. "Webster's gone! So is your bike!"

"I know," Henry said, trying to cover his grin with his hand. "And I'm really sorry. But how cool was that? Just like real stunt kids!"

Keats gave Henry's arm a whack. "How are we going to get anywhere this summer? And what about now? It's too far to walk home without bikes."

Henry shrugged. "No problem. Our moms are still at work. We'll just meet them at the store. They can buy us new bikes on the drive home."

Keats wasn't so sure. But Henry was already heading toward town. Keats rushed to catch up.

It took ten minutes for the cousins to walk to the Purple Rabbit Market, where their moms were cashiers. Like Keats and Henry, their moms were best friends and did everything together. In fact, they looked like twins in their purple uniforms.

Keats's mom spotted the boys when they came into the store. She waved them over to her empty checkout aisle. "How'd you both get so dirty?" she asked.

Henry's mom finished with a customer and joined them. "What's the terrible twosome done now?" she asked, folding her arms.

"Let me do the talking, Keats," Henry whispered. Then, scratching his chin, he started, "Mom and Aunt Marisol, our tale of thrills and chills all started back in—"

Henry's mom held up a hand to stop him. "You better tell us, Keats. We're more likely to get an answer without all the hoopla."

So Keats told them about losing their bikes in the lake. At first their moms were angry. But then they laughed when the cousins asked for money for new bikes. They said the boys would have to find a way to earn the cash themselves.

"But how?" Keats asked.

"I don't know," Keats's mom said sternly. "Now go outside until our shift is over. Without Webster, you'll have to wait for me or Dad to drive you everywhere."

Shuffling his feet, Keats took his time

following Henry out of the store. He missed Webster already. Summer was going to be pretty boring without bikes. When Keats got outside, Henry was standing next to the community message board. It was full of signs that people had pinned up about lost dogs and bake sales.

Henry was smiling again.

"I've solved our problem!" he shouted. He ripped an ad off the board and showed it to Keats. The ad said:

HELP WANTED with ODD JOBS
My house is a disaster!
Looking for someone who can work *real* magic!
Will pay big $$$!

There was an address outside of town and a phone number to leave a message.

"We'll have money for new bikes in no time!" Henry said. "There's a pay phone right there. I'll call and say we'll take the job. It's my new World's Greatest Plan!"

Something about the help-wanted ad struck Keats as weird. He couldn't put his finger on it. "I've got a bad feeling about this," he said.

But, of course, it was too late to stop Henry. He was already dialing the phone.

2

1313 HOUDINI WAY

THWACK! A BRANCH snapped back and smacked Keats in the face.

"Blech," he said, wiping a slimy leaf off his cheek. He couldn't believe he was following Henry on one of his shortcuts. Again.

It was the morning after their bikes had gone into the lake. The cousins were squishing around the swampy woods looking for 1313 Houdini Way. That was the address on the ad.

"Admit it, Henry," Keats said as his sneaker splashed into a pool of muck. "Your *short*cut is a *long*cut. We are so lost. We never should have left the road."

"I know exactly where we are," Henry said. He was scratching his chin, so Keats knew he wasn't telling the truth.

"Okay, where are we?" Keats challenged.

Just then Keats's foot caught on something. He fell forward, his hands scraping on pavement. It was the road! When he looked up, he saw a massive iron gate on the other side. The address on the gate said 1313 Houdini Way.

"We're here!" Henry shouted. He pulled Keats back onto his feet. "See? No problem."

Keats had to smile. Sometimes Henry's plans *did* actually work out.

Past the gate, a long gravel driveway curved around dead trees. A gray house with dark

windows squatted on top of the hill. It looked like a haunted house in a horror movie.

Keats took a step back. "Are you kidding?" he said.

"Come on," Henry said. "Do you want to make money for new bikes or not?"

Tugging Keats along, Henry led the way to the house. They climbed the rickety old steps of the front porch and pressed the doorbell. Instead of a *ding-dong*, there was a buzzing noise. It sounded like *runawayrunaway*. The boys waited. But no one came.

Keats spotted a note taped next to the door. He plucked the note free and read it out loud:

Dear Keats and Henry,

Welcome to Hallway House. Thank you for taking the job. Here are your tasks for today:

• Weed the garden.

- Bring the box of lightbulbs down from the attic.
- Battle and defeat the shark-headed zombie.
- Sweep the garage.

When you're done with everything, I'll return to pay you and take you home.

Sincerely,

Archibald Cigam

P.S. If you need an extra wand, I think there's an old one in the kitchen sink.

"Shark-headed zombie?" Henry said.

"Extra wand?" Keats said.

Henry laughed, and then Keats did, too.

"Well," Henry said, "at least Mr. Cigam knows how to joke around. Come on. Let's start at the top of the list. *Weed the garden.*"

"I didn't see a garden," Keats said, putting Mr. Cigam's note in his pocket. "Did you?"

They looked around. After a couple of minutes they found the "garden." It was a big patch of weeds next to the house.

"Let's get to work," Henry said.

Under the blazing summer sun, the boys started yanking out weeds. They were the really prickly kind with deep roots. They took two hands—or even four—to tug out of the dirt.

With each weed they pulled out, Keats felt the ground shake a little. The first few times he stopped to look around. But after a while he decided the shaking must be his imagination.

Finally the cousins uprooted the last weed. Henry wiped the sweat off his face. "That's done," he said. "What's the next job?"

Keats took out the to-do list to check. Then he froze. A black line was running through the words *weed the garden*. It was as if an invisible pen was crossing it off the list.

"Whoa," Keats said. "Henry, look at this."

But Henry was staring past Keats's shoulder. Keats turned to look, too. About fifty yards away, he spotted a dark triangle sticking up from the ground. It was as high as his knees and moving through the grass.

"What is that?" Keats asked.

"If I didn't know better," Henry said, "I'd say it's a fin."

It *did* look like a fin gliding through the ground.

For a second the fin was all Keats could see. Then a huge mouth popped up out of the grass. Long, sharp teeth crunched down on twigs and rocks.

Some sort of strange creature was swimming through the ground.

It was gobbling up everything in its path. And it was heading straight for the boys!

Henry grabbed Keats's arm and shouted, "Run!"

3

THE SHARK-HEADED ZOMBIE

KEATS DIDN'T MOVE. His eyes wide, he stared at the toothy jaws slicing through the grass and weeds. Keats had never seen anything like this.

It can't be real, Keats thought. Meanwhile, the thing was getting closer.

"Come on!" Henry yanked Keats's arm again. Keats finally snapped out of it. The boys darted across the lawn. They sprinted up the steps of the front porch. Keats almost tripped on the last step. But Henry grabbed him and held him up.

Their hands reached for the front door at the same time. It was locked! The boys pounded on the door and rang the doorbell. But there was no answer.

"I don't get it!" Keats said. "Mr. Cigam gave us jobs to do inside. Why is the door locked?"

"He must have forgotten to leave it open," Henry said. "I think we have bigger problems to deal with than Mr. Cigam's bad memory."

The cousins turned back toward the yard. The creature had followed them! It was halfway between the garden and porch, chewing up all the dirt and stones in its way.

Suddenly the creature stopped. It let out a huge, long burp.

BLLLUURRRP!

"Yuck," Keats said.

Then the thing kept coming. In an instant it was at the porch steps.

"We should have run for the road!" Henry said. "Now we're stuck here!"

The creature took an enormous bite out of the bottom porch step. The wooden step was thick, but it cracked like a toothpick. The boys pressed back against the locked door.

"What *is* that thing?" Keats shouted.

Henry said, "It looks like some kind of shark. But how can a shark swim in grass?"

Shark. That word reminded Keats of the note.

"I bet it's the shark-headed zombie," he said. "Mr. Cigam wasn't kidding!"

When the creature had chewed through the bottom porch step, it stopped again to burp. Then it started crunching on the second step.

Chomp! Crack! Chomp!

Henry jiggled the knob of the locked door. It still wouldn't budge.

The zombie chewed faster as it got closer to the boys. It gnawed on the third step. Just a few feet were left between the cousins and the zombie.

Keats looked around the porch. His mind was racing. "According to *The Big Book of Locks*, three—"

"Oh man! This isn't the library, Keats!" Henry said. "We don't have time for a report on a boring book you just read!"

Keats ignored him. "According to *The Big Book of Locks,* three out of five people leave their keys under the doormat."

Henry rolled his eyes. Keats lifted the doormat. A shiny ring of about ten keys glittered there in the sun.

"Woohoo!" Henry cheered. He slapped

Keats on the back. "I promise never to doubt you again. It's my new World's Greatest Plan."

"Yeah, right," Keats said. But he was smiling, too. Keats picked up the keys and tried one in the lock. The key didn't fit. He tried another.

Henry kept poking him and saying, "Come on! Come on!"

"You're not helping, Henry," Keats muttered. "Just—"

Craaassh! The shark-headed zombie's jagged teeth chomped down on the top step. Its head poked over the edge of the porch. The smell of old fish came from its mouth.

"Hurry!" Henry shouted.

"I'm trying!" Keats chose another key. It didn't fit. Then he tried the last key. It went in smoothly. The door opened with a click. In a rush, Henry and Keats pushed into the house and fell sprawling onto a musty carpet.

Glancing back, Keats saw the shark-headed zombie jump into the air. It was like watching a fish leap out of the water. It did a half-twist and landed on the porch with a thud.

The creature flopped around for a second. Then it got its tail underneath its body and stood up. It looked unsteady, like a seal doing a new trick at the zoo.

The zombie was twice as tall as Keats, and it didn't have just a shark's head. It had flippers for arms, a tail, and black eyes. The thing's skin was smooth and silver like a shark's.

It took a single hop toward the boys.

Keats didn't want to see any more. He slammed the wooden door shut. But Keats knew it wouldn't keep the shark-headed zombie out for long.

"There's an alarm!" Henry said. He was pointing at a big red button on the wall near the door. Keats squinted to read the writing on the button.

"Wait!" Keats shouted. "The button says it's only for emergencies."

"I think this counts," Henry said. Still on his back, he jabbed the button with his foot.

Suddenly a *Whoop! Whoop! Whoop!* filled the house.

"What did you do?" Keats yelled.

The alarm kept ringing. The windows and the front door started to fade. Then they were just gone. In their place was a solid wall.

The cousins were safe from the zombie . . . at least for now.

4

HALLWAY HOUSE

AFTER A FEW seconds the alarm stopped. The house was silent.

"Stunner," Henry said.

Keats and Henry lay on the carpet in the front hall, trying to catch their breath.

"What just happened?" Keats finally said. He stood up slowly. His baseball cap had turned around when he fell. He fixed it and looked around the room.

It was empty except for an old chair and a coatrack in the corner. Keats ran his hand over the wall where the front door used to be. The wall was smooth and solid.

"Where's the door?" Keats asked. "And the windows?"

"I don't know." Henry got to his feet, too. "Probably the alarm made them disappear. You know, to protect whatever is inside the house. It must be some kind of magic."

"That's crazy," Keats said. "There's no such thing as magic—"

Blam! A sudden pounding on the wall next to Keats made him jerk back.

The zombie was on the other side of the wall trying to get inside. *Blam! Blam! Blam!* The wall shook but remained sturdy.

"A shark-headed zombie is on the porch and the front door just vanished," Henry said.

"Ready to change your mind about magic, Keats?"

"Okay, okay," Keats said. "Maybe you're right. Maybe there is magic." His stomach was flip-flopping like crazy.

"Don't panic," Henry said. "It will take time for the zombie to break through. We'll be okay for a while."

Keats looked to see if Henry was scratching his chin. He wasn't. Keats felt a little bit better knowing Henry was telling the truth.

"We need to come up with a plan to get out of the house," Henry said. "Thanks to the alarm, the door and windows are gone. We're trapped."

Keats thought for a second. "I have an idea," he said. He held up the note from Mr. Cigam. "See where Mr. Cigam says he'll take us home when we finish the to-do list?"

Henry snapped his fingers. "That's it! We just have to do all the jobs on the list. And Mr. Cigam will come back and get us out of here."

They both leaned over the note and read the jobs Mr. Cigam had left for them.

- ~~Weed the garden.~~
- Bring the box of lightbulbs down from the attic.
- Battle and defeat the shark-headed zombie.
- Sweep the garage.

"Okay," Keats said. "We weeded the garden. So that's done. The next thing we have to do is bring the lightbulbs down from the attic—"

"And then battle and defeat the shark-headed zombie," Henry said, skipping ahead. "But if the zombie is magical, we'll need magic to fight it. Like a spell. Or maybe a wand—"

"A wand!" Keats said. "At the end of the note, Mr. Cigam says there's an extra wand in the kitchen sink. Where's the kitchen?"

Both boys turned to gaze down the long hallway that led out of the front room. They could see a refrigerator through a doorway at the end of the hall.

"Let's go," Henry said, already moving. Keats followed close on Henry's heels. He couldn't wait to get away from the zombie pounding on the wall.

The instant they left the front room something strange happened.

The doorway they had just passed through shimmered. Then it vanished and became part of the wall. They walked through the next doorway and it happened again. The doorway was gone and a wall stood in its place.

"It must be part of the alarm system,"

Keats said. "I bet every time we go through an opening, it disappears. Just like the front door and the windows. We can't go back the way we came."

"We better stick close together," Henry said. "If I go through a doorway without you and it fades away, we'll be split up."

The boys walked through the last doorway into the kitchen at the same time. They watched that door turn into a wall, too.

The kitchen was messy but looked pretty normal. It had an old stove, a counter stacked with dirty dishes, and the big gray refrigerator. Another door was on the other side of the room.

Keats looked for a phone to call for help. There wasn't one, but he spotted something else. A thick, dusty book sat on the kitchen table. Keats went over to it and read the cover. The book was called *How to Zap Anything*. A

bookmark was stuck inside. Keats flipped to the marked page and read it.

ZAP A ZOMBIE
Step one: Stand on one foot.
Step two: Wave the wand.
Step three: Now say

The rest of step three was gone. The page was torn. It was almost as if something had taken a bite out of it.

"You've got to see this, Henry!" Keats said. "Mr. Cigam found a spell to zap the zombie with the wand. But it's missing the most important part of—"

"Ahhhhh!" Henry interrupted. He was standing by the counter with his back to Keats.

Keats jumped. "What!" he demanded. "What is it now?"

"Oh man. This is just nasty." Henry held up a plate covered in furry mold. "When's the last time Mr. Cigam washed the dishes?"

"You scared me to death." Keats shook his head. "Get serious, Henry. We have to find the wand. It must be in the sink buried under all those dishes."

"What a grouch," Henry said. "Being chased by a zombie must be bad for your funny bone—" Suddenly Henry stopped and shouted, "Ahhhhh!"

This time Keats didn't freak out. "You need some new jokes, Henry."

"Uh, Keats," Henry said quietly. It was the voice he used when he didn't want Keats to panic. "I think *you* found the sink."

"Oh yeah?" Keats wasn't going to fall for one of Henry's pranks. "What makes you say that?"

"Because you're standing in it," Henry said. "Look at your feet."

Keats did. Or tried to. He couldn't see his feet. They were gone!

His sneakers had been sucked into the kitchen floor like it was quicksand.

"I'm sinking!" Keats shouted.

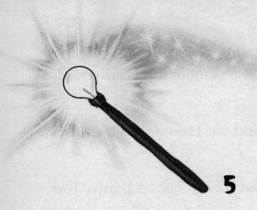

5

THE KITCHEN SINK

KEATS TRIED TO pull his feet free. But he couldn't budge. If anything, struggling only made him sink faster. The floor quickly rose to his shins. Soon he would be sucked all the way down.

Henry and the rest of the room were still on solid ground. This was the only part of the kitchen with a squishy spot.

"That must be what Mr. Cigam's note meant

by the kitchen *sink*," Henry said. "It's some kind of sinkhole."

The floor was up to Keats's knees now. It was like sliding into taffy. "Henry, help me!" he yelled.

Thinking fast, Henry tied two crusty dish towels together and tossed one end to Keats. He grabbed it and Henry pulled. Just as Keats started to climb up, his foot bumped into something.

"There's something jammed in here," Keats said.

With one hand still on the towel rope, Keats reached into the spongy floor. There was a *gurgle* as he yanked out a small scepter, like a king might carry. Only this one had a lightbulb screwed into the top.

Keats flung the rod to Henry. He put it on the counter so he could keep pulling.

But crawling out of the sinkhole was getting harder. When Keats had tugged the rod free, it was like unclogging the drain in a bathtub. Things started going down the hole faster. The floor began to swirl a little as it spun around Keats.

The moving floor made the table tip over. Still open to the marked page, the *How to Zap Anything* book fell and skidded toward the pit.

"The spell!" Keats let go of the rope with one hand again. He reached for the book. But he was only able to grab one page. The page ripped off in his fingers and the rest of the book was sucked into the hole.

There was a *shuuuwmack* sound. Suddenly everything stopped swirling. With Henry's help, Keats pulled himself onto solid ground.

"The book must have plugged up the hole again," Keats said, getting to his feet. He uncrumpled the torn page in his hand. "But I saved the spell!"

"Great job, Keats," Henry said, and picked up the rod on the counter. "Do you think this is the wand Mr. Cigam was talking about?"

Keats eyed it. "I thought a magic wand would look different. This is just a goofy stick with a lightbulb on top." He shrugged. "But in this house, that's weird enough to be right."

"Good point," Henry agreed.

BLAM! The boys jumped as pounding started on the wall behind the counter.

Keats began to panic again. "The zombie is trying to break into the house! It's right on the other side of that wall!"

Henry tried to calm him down. "That works out great," he said. "We can try out the wand and the spell you found."

Keats took a deep breath, then nodded. "It's only part of the spell, but what do we have to lose?" he said. "After all, it's called Zap a Zombie."

The boys faced the wall where the zombie was pounding. Keats held the spell, and Henry held the wand.

"Okay," Keats said. "Step one says we have to stand on one foot." The boys did. Keats was a little more wobbly than Henry.

Keats read step two. "Now wave the wand."

Henry did. "What's next?"

"I don't know," Keats answered. "We're supposed to say something. But step three is missing. I don't know what the words are."

"You named your bike after the guy who wrote the dictionary," Henry said. "You like words! Make something up!"

Keats thought for a second. "How about . . . zombie, go up a tree and set us free!"

"That's really strange," Henry said with a nod. "But I like it."

Henry waved the wand, and both boys said, "Zombie, go up a tree and set us free!"

Keats held his breath. Henry was grinning, waiting for a bang or something big.

But nothing happened. The zombie just kept ramming the wall. The boys put both feet on the floor again.

"Sorry," Keats said, disappointed. "We
need the real words to make the spell work."

"It's not just that. Listen." Henry shook the
wand again. Keats heard a rattling sound. It
was the noise a burned-out lightbulb makes.

Keats said, "The bulb is burned out. The wand probably can't work with a busted bulb."

"No problem," said Henry. "We'll just get another one."

But it was a problem. They looked in the cabinets. There weren't any bulbs there. And the ones in the lamps in the kitchen were all too big. They didn't fit into the wand.

"Hold on!" Henry said. "I know where we can find a bulb. In the note, Mr. Cigam asked us to *bring the box of lightbulbs down from the attic.* The bulbs are waiting for us! We just have to go get them."

Keats felt his stomach flip-flop.

If the garden and the kitchen were so creepy, he could only imagine how scary the attic would be.

6

DETOUR!

"WAIT A SECOND, Henry," Keats said. "I just want to make sure I understand your new World's Greatest Plan." He took a deep breath and asked, "You want us to go up to the attic to get the lightbulbs and bring them downstairs and use one of them to put in the wand so we can zap the zombie with a spell and finish the to-do list so the owner of the house will come back and take us home?"

Henry laughed at the really long question. He knew Keats was trying to stall. "Don't go chicken on me, Keats. We can follow my plan. Or we can stay here and wait for our zombie pal."

Keats looked at the shaking kitchen wall. The pounding from outside had gotten louder. Cracks were forming in the wall. It wouldn't be long before the zombie broke through.

"Okay, let's go," Keats said.

Henry opened the door on the other side of the room. Behind the door was a hallway.

"*Another* hallway?" Keats asked.

Henry shrugged. "I guess that's why Mr. Cigam called this place Hallway House."

The hallway was fairly dark. Doors lined both walls. And at the end, they could make out the bottom steps of a winding staircase.

"Those steps must lead up to the attic," Henry said. "Come on."

With Keats holding the wand, the boys crept out of the kitchen. After they walked through the doorway, it shimmered. Then it was gone. This seemed totally normal by now. But it also made the hallway even darker.

Slowly, the boys made their way down the hall.

"Ouch!" a voice said.

Henry chuckled. "What's wrong now, Keats?"

"I didn't say anything," Keats said.

"Then who said 'ouch'?" Henry asked.

"I thought you did," Keats said. He took another step.

"Ouch!" a voice said again. Something nipped at Keats's toes. He could feel it through his sneaker. He jerked back his foot. "What was that?" Keats asked in shock.

"It's too dark," Henry said. "I can't tell."

Keats pressed the button for the light on his watch. He aimed the light down at the carpet.

"There are faces on the rug!" Keats yelled. In the dim light from his watch, he could see the pattern in the carpet. Faces as big as oranges had been woven into the fabric.

The faces were repeated over and over. There was one about every three inches—and they were moving!

Blinking, yawning, frowning. Each face was like the head of a stick figure. They just had eyes and mouths and looked like something a little kid might draw.

Henry crouched down and touched one of the faces.

"Ouch!" the face cried. It bit Henry's finger. He pulled his hand back.

"I don't think they have teeth, but that still hurts!" Henry said. "Why would Mr. Cigam want a carpet like this?"

"Maybe the faces are like the zombie, and he doesn't want them here," Keats said. "What are we going to do? We can't go back. And we can't get to the attic steps without stepping on the faces."

Henry frowned and then snapped his fingers. "Sure we can!" he announced. "Just walk on your toes. Like this." Henry stood up on the tips of his shoes and stepped forward. As Henry moved, he put his toes in the empty spaces between the faces.

Henry tiptoed farther down the hall. "Come on, Keats! It's kind of like dancing."

That was the problem. Keats wasn't a very good dancer. But he didn't have a choice.

Keats got up on his toes. He looked down

and started walking carefully on the carpet. His eyes were used to the dark now. As Keats stepped between the faces, they watched him. A couple opened their mouths. They were ready to bite him if he stepped too close.

That made it even harder to think about what he was doing. Keats started tiptoeing faster. Soon he was moving so quickly, he couldn't stop. If he did, he'd fall over.

Waving the wand in front of him, Keats pushed past Henry and almost tripped both of them. Then he started to mess up.

"Ouch!" said a face on the carpet as Keats stepped on it.

"Ouch!" said Keats as the face bit his toe.

"Ouch!" another face shouted, and bit down.

"Ouch!" Keats cried again.

The hall filled with shouts of "Ouch!" from the faces and Keats.

"Almost there!" Henry called over the racket. "Keep going!"

The boys were just a few feet away from the attic stairs. But Keats couldn't make it. A face bit down especially hard on his toe. Keats finally lost his balance and fell sideways.

"Ack!" Keats yelled. He tumbled through a doorway. The wrong doorway.

Henry didn't have a choice. He had to follow Keats or they would be separated.

"I'm coming, Keats!" Henry shouted.

And before the door could disappear, Henry dove after him.

7

THE BOOKWORMS

THE COUSINS ROLLED through the doorway, across the room's hard floor, and banged to a stop against a bookshelf.

Once again, Keats and Henry found themselves lying on their backs, trying to catch their breath.

"Where are we?" Henry asked, sitting up.

Keats sat up, too. Luckily, he had managed to hold on to the wand. He looked around the room. Bookshelves climbed up the high walls. Weird railings that looked like thick tubes wove in and out of the shelves.

"It's a library," Keats said. He was still a little dizzy from all the tumbling.

Henry looked pretty unhappy. "Well, I'm glad we're in one of your favorite places," he said. "Because we're trapped."

It was true. The door to the hallway had become a wall after they fell through it. And there wasn't a single door or window in the room.

Keats felt lousy. "I'm sorry, Henry. We were so close to the attic and getting the lightbulb! I just couldn't keep my balance."

Henry gave him a smile. "Hey, don't worry about it, Keats," he said. "I wanted a tour of the house anyway."

Keats smiled, too. Then he thought of

something. "In books," he said, "libraries in creepy houses always have secret passages."

Henry frowned. "Secret passages?"

"Sure, you know, hidden doorways," Keats said. "We just have to pull on the right book, and I bet a way out will open up."

"There are thousands of books in here," Henry said. "But it can't hurt to try."

The cousins got to their feet. They started sliding books on and off the nearest shelf. Nothing happened.

Maybe one of the books on the higher shelves would do the trick. Keats climbed up onto one of the wide railings. It was a little soft but held his weight.

Keats pulled on book after book. Still no sign of a secret door. Suddenly the railing he was standing on started to move. It twisted and turned under his feet.

Keats dropped the book in his hand. He jumped down to the floor.

"Was that an earthquake?" Keats asked.

"More like an earth*worm*," Henry said. "A big one."

He pointed at what Keats had thought was a railing. The thick tube was sliding around with squishy, glooping sounds.

"That's not an earthworm. It's a giant book-worm!" Keats cried.

As if to prove Keats right, the worm pulled its head out of a nearby book. It didn't have eyes or ears. But its mouth was as wide as a watermelon. The worm chomped down on another book. It tore off part of the cover and chewed slowly, like a cow with a mouthful of grass.

Keats looked around the library again. There were at least six more giant bookworms tunneling through the books. Each one was as long as a minivan. They must have gone still when the boys burst into the room. But now they seemed to realize the cousins weren't a threat and went back to eating.

And as they ate they made gassy sounds like *Gloop! Shoolllop!*

"Oh man," Keats said. He pinched his nose.

"That's totally disgusting," Henry agreed. "They don't look dangerous. Unless they want to *stink* us to death."

Keats started to put back the book he'd dropped. Then he noticed the title.

"*Spells—No Wand Needed,*" he read out loud.

"Great!" Henry said. He took the book and flipped to the middle. "Let's try one. It could help us get out of here. This spell sounds good. It's called Egg-cellent Idea!"

"Wait a second," Keats said. "We shouldn't mess around with this stuff."

But it was too late. Henry was already reading the spell. " 'Put the cluck right up there or the yolk will hit our hair!' "

Blip! A live chicken popped into the air in the middle of the library. It was about six feet off the ground. It clucked and laid an egg. Henry stuck out his hand and caught the egg before it hit the ground. Flapping its wings, the chicken fluttered to the floor.

"Are you seeing what I'm seeing?" Henry asked. "I just made a chicken appear out of thin air! How cool is that?"

The chicken started strutting around the library, pecking at the floor. It clucked again. Then, with a *blip!,* the chicken vanished.

Keats took the egg from Henry. "Well, when we want an omelet, we'll know what to do. But how is that spell going to help us against the zombie?"

"Okay, you're right," Henry said. "Let's find another one."

Before they could look for a more useful spell—

Ker-thunk! Crash!

Keats dropped the egg in surprise. It smashed on the floor.

"What was that noise?" he asked.

"That was the sound of a hole being made in the kitchen wall," Henry said. "You know what that means?"

For a second Keats couldn't talk. He knew exactly what that sound meant.

The shark-headed zombie was inside the house!

8

ESCAPE FROM THE LIBRARY

THROUGH THE WALLS, Keats heard the zombie banging around the kitchen. Pots and pans clattered. Glasses shattered. Then there was a huge *WHAM!* that made him jump. Keats figured it was the refrigerator being tipped over.

Henry and Keats looked at each other with wide eyes. Up until this moment, they had felt safe from the zombie. But now it was inside the house with them.

Henry finally said, "If the zombie breaks through the walls and gets in here—"

"We'll be sitting ducks." Keats finished the sentence for him. "We have to get out of this library."

Henry nodded. "But how? There was just that one door. And it's gone."

Keats slid a few books off a nearby shelf.

"We tried that, Keats," Henry said a little sharply. "Yanking on books isn't going to open a secret passage."

"I have a new idea," Keats said. He pulled out another book. This one had been half eaten by the worms. The cover was ripped off. The pages inside were shredded. Keats grabbed a handful of torn pages. He waved them at one end of the nearest worm.

"What are you doing?" Henry asked.

Keats didn't answer. He dangled the pages

like bait. Then he started talking to the worm. "Mmmmm, delicious book juice," he crooned.

Henry chuckled. "If you're looking for the worm's face, you're at the wrong end."

Keats blushed. He went to the other end of the worm, which was half buried in a book. Keats shook the torn pages in the air again.

The worm pulled its head out of the book and sniffed the air. It smelled the pages. Then Keats rubbed them on the wall next to the worm.

"Come and get it, wormy!" Keats said softly.

Gloob. With yet another gassy sound, the bookworm wriggled to the wall. Its mouth opened wide. The worm took a huge bite out of the wall, right where Keats had rubbed the pages.

Instantly the worm's whole body shook. It spit out the pieces of the wall on the floor.

Plaster, wood, and a few chewed-up pages
dribbled out of its mouth. Keats could imagine the worm thinking, "Gross!"

Henry said, "I bet that's how I look when I
eat my mom's tuna surprise."

"Pretty much," Keats agreed with a laugh.

The worm slithered higher up the bookshelf to find a better meal. And the boys were left looking at a pile of bookworm vomit and a hole in the wall. The hole wasn't big. But the boys could squeeze through it and get out of the library!

Henry slapped Keats on the back. "Great job, cuz," Henry said. "And sorry. I did it again. I doubted that you'd find something in a book to help us."

Keats smiled. "No big deal, Henry."

Without waiting another second, the boys crawled over what the worm had thrown up and went into the hole together. Three words on a scrap of paper in the goop caught Keats's eye.

". . . zap the zombie . . ."

He plucked it out of the gunk and kept going.

Once they were through, the hole closed up behind them, just like the doorways. But it didn't matter. They were back in the hall. Careful to avoid the faces in the carpet, they got to their feet.

Keats wiped the scrap of paper on his pants. "Look! That worm must be the one who took a bite out of the *How to Zap Anything* book. This is the missing part of the spell!"

Keats held the scrap next to the page from the book in the kitchen. Like two puzzle pieces, they fit perfectly. "For step three, we say, 'Pause the snapping jaws and zap the zombie from IS to WAS!'"

"We have the rest of the spell?" Henry asked.

"Right," Keats said. "But we still need the lightbulb to fix the wand. We've got to get up to the attic."

Keats glanced back toward the kitchen. The wall where the kitchen door had stood was shaking. The zombie was breaking through it. They didn't have long.

The cousins headed quickly toward the spiral staircase at the other end of the hall. This time they didn't bother trying to tiptoe. They just ran. Their feet smooshed the faces in the carpet.

"Ouch! Ouch! Ouch!" the faces cried.

The faces tried to bite their toes, but the boys were moving too fast.

"Sorry! Sorry! Sorry!" Keats and Henry told them.

When they reached the winding staircase, they raced up to the gloomy, dusty attic.

There were no windows, but light came through small cracks in the roof. Keats brushed cobwebs out of his eyes.

It was like Keats's attic at home, but about ten times bigger and jammed full of all sorts of junk. Boxes were everywhere. Old clothes hung on racks. There was even a rusting suit of knight's armor in the far corner.

"Let's hunt down that box of bulbs," Henry said. He took a step. There was a scary creaking sound. "Be careful, Keats," he said. "The floor is rotting. We don't want to end up on top of the zombie thing below."

The boys split up. Keats took one side of the attic and Henry took the other. They moved slowly at first, worried they might crash through the floor.

Then another loud smashing sound came from downstairs.

"The zombie is in the hallway," Henry said. "I think it's trying to get through that last wall at the bottom of the stairs."

"We have to find the lightbulbs NOW!" shouted Keats.

Henry and Keats stopped being careful and raced around the attic. They yanked open boxes and pawed through them. Keats pulled out the drawers in a wobbly dresser. He found a few old toy cars. They were pretty cool but wouldn't help them now.

"Whoa!" Henry cried from across the room. Keats turned to see what was wrong. Somehow Henry had gotten tangled up in an old dress. He tripped and fell. Dust flew into the air and the floor creaked under him again.

"What's this?" Henry asked. He had landed right next to a box in the corner. On the side of the box were the words LUXE WAND LIGHT-BULBS.

Henry tore free from the dress. "I found it!" he shouted.

Of course! Keats thought with a smile. *Only Henry could trip over a dress and still have everything work out.*

Keats unscrewed the bad lightbulb from the wand. "I can put in a new bulb. And we can use it to zap the zombie. Hurry!"

Henry took a step forward. He was about to hand the box to Keats when—

The weak floor under Henry caved in. The rotting wood tore like paper. Henry dropped through the hole, taking the box of bulbs with him.

Keats rushed to the edge of the hole. Luckily, Mr. Cigam had left a ratty old bed in the middle of the dirty garage below. Keats was just in time to see Henry land on it with a bounce. Keats heard lightbulbs in the box breaking.

"Keats!" Henry called up to him. "You have to jump through the hole before it disa—"

Too late. The hole in the attic floor shimmered and sealed shut. The boys were now separated.

Keats was alone. But he wouldn't be for long.

He could hear the *chomp, chomp, chomp* of the shark-headed zombie at the bottom of the stairs.

In just a few seconds the zombie would break into the attic.

9

KEATS'S SURPRISE

WHEN THE ZOMBIE burst into the room, Keats knew he was in big trouble.

From his hiding place, Keats held the wand and watched the zombie hop around the attic on its tail. It looked kind of like a clumsy jack-in-the-box. Normally Keats would have laughed. But silly-looking or not, the zombie was dangerous. It would probably like to make a meal out of him.

On top of everything, the zombie stank like fish. Fish that had been sitting out in the hot sun for a couple of days.

Keats forced himself not to gag. Seriously, the thing needed a bar of soap and a good toothbrush.

Now would be the perfect time for Keats to zap the zombie. But he couldn't. He needed a lightbulb to make the wand work. And all the lightbulbs were with Henry down in the garage.

The zombie hopped again, and then it froze. Its eyes were locked on Keats's baseball cap in the corner of the attic. Then it spotted Keats's jacket!

With two quick hops, it bounced closer.

The zombie lifted the arm of Keats's jacket.

"Wait," Keats whispered to himself. "Don't move yet."

The zombie bit down on the jacket. There was a clang as the zombie's teeth struck metal.

"Mrrrrhhhs!" The zombie moaned in pain. It sounded hurt and confused.

Keats's trick had worked!

Just before the zombie had broken into the attic, Keats had come up with a plan. He had put his baseball cap and jacket on the suit of armor. Meanwhile, he had hidden behind a box across the attic.

The zombie was really angry now. With a flipper, it touched its sore mouth. Then it shoved the suit of armor like a bully pushing a kid on the playground. The armor rocked back and forth. It toppled on the zombie, trapping it against the wall.

"Now!" Keats told himself. He leapt out from behind the box.

The zombie saw Keats and let out an angry burp. But it was stuck under the heavy armor.

Keats looked for the spot where the floor seemed the most rotten. He jumped as high as he could. Then his feet hit the floor. With a giant *crack!*, the old boards gave way. Keats plunged through the attic floor.

He landed hard on a thick shag rug in the room below. His legs buckled and he fell to his knees. But he was okay, and so was the wand.

Keats must have picked the wrong spot on the floor of the attic. He had hoped to end up in the garage with Henry. Instead he was in a living room. A huge television from around 1965 filled one corner, and a big orange couch sat across from it. Through an open door, Keats saw the hallway with the weird faces on the carpet. On the other side of the room was a second door. It was closed.

How could he get to the garage?

Keats was just getting to his feet when he heard the zombie up in the attic. It was throwing aside the suit of armor.

Oh no! Keats looked up at the hole he had

made. It was closing. At that instant the zombie dove headfirst toward Keats.

Keats pressed down into the rug, waiting for the zombie to land on him. But it never did.

The zombie had jerked to a stop. It was hanging upside down in the air, just inches above Keats. The zombie's flapping flippers couldn't quite reach him. Neither could its snapping jaws.

What happened? Keats wondered as he slid from under the zombie. Then he saw the answer.

The hole had closed around the zombie's tail! It had trapped the zombie like a wriggling trout on a hook.

There was no time for a victory dance. The zombie was curling up toward the ceiling and pounding on it with its flippers. It would break free before long.

Keats had two choices. He could go out
the open door to the hallway with the weird
face carpet. But that way could be a dead end.

After all, the attic, kitchen, and library were all sealed up.

Or he could try the closed door on the other side of the room. But that meant passing pretty close to the zombie.

The zombie was almost loose. Keats would only have time to choose one door.

Be like Henry, Keats thought. *Take a chance. Try the closed door.*

Holding his breath against the fish smell, he inched along the wall and past the upside-down zombie. The creature was too busy flapping at the ceiling to notice him.

Keats reached the small door and opened it. "Yes!" he said. It was another hallway!

He stepped through the door just as the zombie jerked out of the ceiling.

Keats turned to see the zombie and pieces of the ceiling fall to the shag rug. *Boing!* The zombie was up in a flash, bouncing toward Keats.

At the last second, though, the zombie stopped. It cocked its head, looking at the doorway, which was now shimmering. Keats could tell the zombie didn't want to get stuck again. It wasn't going to risk coming through just as the doorway was becoming a wall.

Since he was safe, Keats couldn't resist doing something else Henry might do. He gave the zombie a funny salute and said, "Better luck next time!"

The zombie let out a frustrated burp and waved its flippers angrily. Then the doorway vanished. A wall separated the zombie and Keats.

He laughed. He had done it. He had escaped the zombie!

Now he just had to keep his fingers crossed

that this hall led to the garage. Keats hurried down the dark passageway. As he went, he opened different doors. There were closets and a bathroom. But no garage.

He opened the last door. It was the garage!

And, even better, Henry was there. With his back to Keats, he was standing on the middle of the bed. Right where he'd landed when he fell from the attic.

Keats was so happy to see his cousin. He burst in without looking at anything else. The door behind him vanished. And so did Keats's smile.

"Rats," he said.

Keats wished he had looked more carefully before rushing into the garage.

Why?

Because the shark-headed zombie was already there.

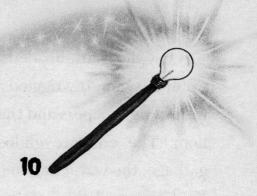

10

THE BATTLE OF THE GARAGE

WHILE KEATS HAD been running down that last hallway, the zombie must have gone back up to the attic. Then it had busted through the attic floor to the garage!

Now the zombie was circling Henry, coming closer and closer to the bed. Standing up on the mattress, Henry looked as if he was stuck on a raft with a hungry shark swimming around him.

Only the shark-headed zombie didn't need water to swim. It wriggled on its belly through the old newspapers and trash that covered the floor. The creature glided smoothly in the garbage, the way it had in the ground outside. Keats guessed this was easier for it than all that clumsy hopping.

"Henry!" Keats called. "Are you okay?"

At the sound of Keats's voice, the zombie

glanced his way. Keats scrambled up onto a nearby workbench. But the zombie didn't come after him. It seemed to be having too much fun scaring Henry. And it just kept circling the bed.

Henry turned around. He held two light-bulbs. "Keats!" Henry said with a big smile. "Wow, am I glad to see you!"

"Me too," Keats said. "Why didn't you get out of the garage when you had the chance?"

"I couldn't," Henry answered. "My foot got stuck in a mattress spring when I hit the bed. I just got it free when that thing showed up."

As if hearing its name, the zombie's head popped out of the trash. Its jaws snapped in the air near Henry.

"Watch out!" Keats yelled.

Henry threw a lightbulb at the zombie. It ducked back under the garbage. And the bulb shattered against a rusty lawn mower.

"I've been holding the zombie back with the lightbulbs," Henry explained. "It's scared of them for some reason. But most of them broke when I fell."

Keats nodded. "Toss me the lightbulb!" he shouted. "I'll put it in the wand and say the spell."

Up on the workbench, he was about fifteen feet away from Henry.

"Okay," Henry said. "But don't drop it! It's the last one."

Henry got ready for a throw. Just then the shark-headed zombie bumped the bed. If Henry had thrown the bulb, it would have shattered on the floor.

Henry was about to try another toss when the zombie rammed the bed again. This time it hit the bed so hard that Henry fell over on the mattress. He quickly got back to his feet.

"Did the bulb break?" Keats asked.

"No, it's okay," Henry said. "But the zombie isn't going to let me get a good throw."

"All right," Keats said. "I'll toss the wand to you."

At that moment the zombie leapt into the air between Henry and Keats. Its mouth opened and closed with a *clack*. It hit the floor and kept wriggling around the bed.

"Don't throw the wand!" Henry shouted. "The zombie will catch it. I think it can understand what we're saying."

Keats's mind raced. Without the bulb he couldn't make the wand work. What could they do?

The zombie's circles grew even smaller. Now it was chewing through the edges of the mattress. Bits of stuffing and feathers flew into the air. The garage looked like the site of a crazy pillow fight.

Trying to keep his balance on the bed, Henry bounced from foot to foot. Meanwhile, Keats's brain bounced from idea to idea.

But he didn't say any of the ideas out loud. Especially now that he knew the zombie could understand words.

The boys were running out of time. Soon the zombie would eat more of the bed and

Henry would be in big trouble. Then the cousins looked right at each other. And a silent idea passed between them.

After a second Henry said, "I've got a new World's Greatest Plan." He made his voice sound sad. "I'm just going to stay right here and not try to get away."

The zombie heard this and slowed down. It reminded Keats of a cat that wants to toy with a mouse a little longer.

But there was one thing the zombie didn't notice, or just didn't understand. Keats saw it, though.

Henry was scratching his chin.

Keats hoped they both had the same plan. To be sure, he asked, "I guess you're the one who is *chicken* now?"

Henry nodded and got ready.

At the same time, the boys said, "Put the

cluck right up there or the yolk will hit our hair!"

Blip! Blip! Two chickens popped into the air over the zombie. Flapping their wings, the

chickens laid eggs that fell and smashed on the zombie's face. For the moment it couldn't see a thing.

Henry moved like a flash. He leapt off the bed, jumping over the zombie. Henry landed next to the workbench and climbed up next to Keats. The chickens fluttered to the floor and vanished with two more clucks.

"Egg-cellent job, cuz," Keats said.

Henry rolled his eyes at the joke and handed over the bulb. Keats screwed it into the wand.

The zombie wiped a flipper over its eyes, clearing away the egg yolk. It realized that Henry was no longer on the bed. The zombie turned and spotted the boys together.

Like lightning, it wriggled toward them, its jaws opening and clacking shut.

"Let's say the spell!" Keats shouted. "Now!"

The boys both put a hand on the wand and stood on one foot. They waved the wand at the zombie.

Together they said, "Pause the snapping jaws and zap the zombie from IS to WAS!"

The zombie was just inches away. They waited a heartbeat for something to happen—

And this time something did.

Kablam!

A bright light shot out of the wand, knocking the boys back against the wall. The light hit the zombie with a sizzling sound.

There was a rush of air, too. It was as if someone had just opened a window in the middle of a hurricane.

The boys squeezed their eyes shut against the blast. When they opened them, the creature was gone.

The shark-headed zombie had been zapped!

11

MR. CIGAM

THE COUSINS GAVE each other high fives.

"We did it!" Henry said. But Keats could barely hear him.

The wind created by the blast from the wand still howled around the garage. Swirling from dusty corner to dusty corner, the whirlwind grew into a small tornado. It was as tall as Henry.

The tornado whipped past Henry and

Keats, tugging at them. But they clung to the workbench.

As it spun around the garage, the tornado sucked in all the dirt, the garbage, the chicken eggs, the dead leaves, and even the chewed-up mattress. All the while, the tornado was blowing up like a balloon being stretched too tight.

With a *pop!* the tornado vanished. The garage was suddenly silent.

The boys climbed off the workbench. They looked around with wide eyes. The garage glittered. The tornado had taken all the dirt and garbage with it. It was as if a crew had swept through and cleaned every inch of the garage.

"Stunner," Henry said.

Keats pulled out the to-do list.

- ~~Weed the garden.~~
- ~~Bring the box of lightbulbs down from the attic.~~

- ~~Battle and defeat the shark-headed zombie.~~
- Sweep the garage.

Lines had been drawn through the top three things on the list. Keats watched as a line ran through the last one.

- ~~Sweep the garage.~~

"We're done, Henry!" Keats said. "We've finished every job on the list!"

Just then a wall in the garage shimmered. A garage door appeared and started to roll up with a rattle.

Bright summer sunshine flooded into the garage. The boys squinted against the light and made their way outside.

"Look," Henry said. "Someone's coming."

They stood at the top of the driveway,

watching a car rumble toward them. It was a long black limousine.

"Check it out," Henry said. "There's no one driving."

"Why doesn't that surprise me?" Keats said.

The limo with no driver pulled up next to the boys. A window in the back rolled down. An old man's face peeked out. He had a pointy white beard under his chin and a pointy white patch of hair on top of his head. It made his face look kind of like a diamond.

"Hello, Henry and Keats!" the man said in a friendly voice.

"Are you Mr. Cigam?" Henry asked.

"That's right." The man nodded. "And Hallway House is my house. I told you I would return when the work was done. And here I am."

Keats had so many questions. He didn't know where to start. "Are you a magician?" he asked.

"I used to be a great magician," Mr. Cigam said. He shrugged. "Sorry to say, my magic is not what it once was. I've been feeling a little backward lately. And so has Hallway House. It was once filled with so many wonderful things!"

"Now it's pretty scary," Henry said.

Mr. Cigam nodded. "I'm trying to fix that. That's why I put up an ad for people who could work real magic."

"Wait a second," Henry said. "When you said 'looking for someone who can work real magic'—"

"You meant *real* magic!" Keats finished the sentence.

"Of course," Mr. Cigam said. "And I can

see you boys worked hard. Here's the payment I promised you."

The man stuck a bony hand out the limo's window. He flipped a coin into the air. Henry caught it.

One coin? Keats felt his good mood sink. After all they had gone through for new bikes, they were getting a coin? They couldn't even buy a spoke for a wheel with that.

"Hold the phone," Henry said. He was staring at the coin. "That's gold!"

Keats took a closer look. It *was* gold!

They could buy the best bikes in the world and still have money left over. Then Keats imagined what their parents would say.

"We can't take this," Keats said. "On top of everything else, your house is still pretty messy. Especially the kitchen."

"Pish," Mr. Cigam said. "Of course you can

take it. I gave you tough jobs to do. That pesky shark-headed zombie made my life miserable for months. You earned it."

Keats thought for a second. It was true. They had been in real danger. He had lost his baseball cap and jacket in the attic. And they had completed everything on the to-do list. Maybe they did deserve the money.

Mr. Cigam and Henry waited for his decision.

"Okay, we'll take it," Keats announced. "Thank you."

"Yes!" Henry said. He pumped his fist in the air.

Keats laughed. "Well . . ." He didn't know how to say goodbye to a magician. Was there a special goodbye spell or something? This question about magic reminded Keats that he was still holding the wand.

"Oh!" Keats said. "I almost forgot to give this back. Here."

He tried to hand the wand to Mr. Cigam.

"What? That old thing?" the old man said, waving it away. "You boys can keep the wand. Just promise to use it properly."

Henry's eyes widened. Keats knew what Henry was thinking. He was picturing how he could use the wand to make all of his World's Greatest Plans come true. Like the one about becoming Hollywood stunt kids.

"I promise to use it the right way," Henry said. There was a gleam in his eye. And he was scratching his chin.

With a grin, Keats said, "I think I better hold on to the wand for now."

Mr. Cigam clapped his hands together. "Well, that's all settled. Now hop in. I'll give you two a ride home."

Stepping back, Henry took another look at the limo with no driver. "Honestly, I've had enough magic for one day," he said.

"Me too," Keats agreed. "I guess we'll walk. But thanks anyway, Mr. Cigam."

The boys said goodbye and walked down the driveway. Mr. Cigam waved out the limo's window. He called after them, "I'll let you know if any other odd jobs come up!"

"That'd be great!" Henry called back.

Keats waited until they were on the road. Then he asked, "Would you really take another job with Mr. Cigam, Henry?"

"I told him I'd had enough magic for today," Henry said. "But there's always tomorrow!"

ABOUT THE AUTHOR

BILL DOYLE grew up in Michigan and wrote his first story—a funny whodunit—when he was eight. Since then, he's written other action-packed books for kids, like *Everest: You Decide How to Survive,* the Crime Through Time series, and the Behind Enemy Lines series. He lives in New York City with two dachshund-headed dogs.

You can visit him online at billdoyle.net.

Don't miss Keats and Henry's
next adventure!

STAMPEDE
OF THE
SUPERMARKET
SLUGS